This book belongs to

_____

Barbie™
in
The Troll's Bridge

Illustrations by Lawrence Mann

EGMONT

First published in Great Britain 2009
by Egmont UK Limited
239 Kensington High Street, London W8 6SA

BARBIE and associated trademarks and trade dress are owned by,
and used under licence from, Mattel, Inc.
© 2009 Mattel, Inc.

ISBN 978 1 4052 4433 6

1 3 5 7 9 10 8 6 4 2

Printed in Germany

The Forest Stewardship Council (FSC) is an international, non-governmental organisation dedicated to promoting responsible
management of the world's forests. FSC operates a system of forest certification and product labelling that allows consumers to
identify wood and wood-based products from well managed forests.

For more information about Egmont's paper buying policy please visit www.egmont.co.uk/ethicalpublishing
For more information about the FSC please visit their website at www.fsc.uk.org

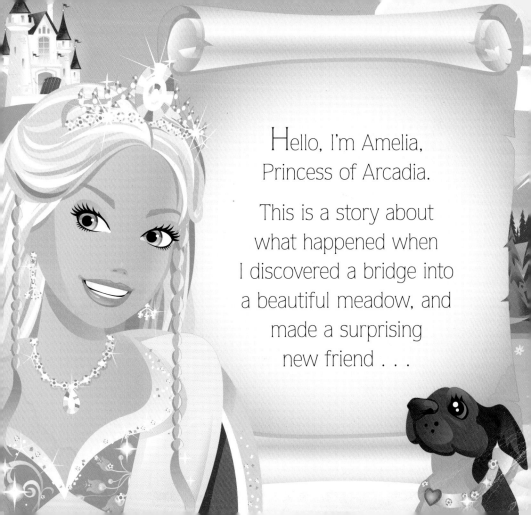

Hello, I'm Amelia,
Princess of Arcadia.

This is a story about
what happened when
I discovered a bridge into
a beautiful meadow, and
made a surprising
new friend . . .

Princess Amelia was playing ball with Truffle in the royal garden. The two friends chased each other here and there, and Amelia laughed gleefully as Truffle yapped with joy.

As they ran to the very end of the royal garden, Amelia saw something she had not noticed before. A rickety footbridge crossed the babbling brook into a lush meadow. "I wonder who put that bridge there?" she said.

The meadow was as pretty as a picture, sunny and bright, full of blossom trees and wild flowers, and heavy with the scent of honey.

"What a lovely meadow," gasped Amelia. "It would be the perfect place for a summer ball!"

Truffle was watching a flock of woolly lambs leaping in the long grass of the meadow. He wanted to play, too. Before Amelia could stop him, Truffle had scampered over the bridge into the sunny meadow, past rotting wooden signs that read, "No trespassers! Beware of the troll!" and "Mean troll! Keep out!"

"Come back, Truffle," Amelia cried, running after him, her shoes trip-trapping on the wooden planks of the bridge.

Suddenly, from beneath the bridge, a voice growled at Amelia, "Who's that trip-trapping over MY bridge?"

"I – I'm Princess Amelia!" she replied in a shaky voice, "and I'm coming to fetch my little dog back."

The whole bridge rattled, and a troll appeared in front of Amelia, with a long, warty nose, crooked teeth and very tatty clothes.

But as the troll stomped towards Amelia, he stubbed his big toe on a loose plank of wood. He howled and hopped, making the rickety bridge wobble from side to side.

"Here, let me help you!" cried Amelia, bending to pull a splinter from the troll's toe.

"Hmmph. Thank you," said the troll gruffly. Then he plodded into the meadow, scooped up Truffle and, holding the little dog by the scruff of his neck, handed him back to Amelia. "Now, go away and don't come back! This is MY bridge. Clodhopper's bridge and Clodhopper's meadow!"

But the next day, Amelia and Truffle found themselves near the bridge once more, playing with their golden ball. Suddenly, the ball bounced up and over the bridge.

"What's that bouncing over my bridge?" growled Clodhopper, who was hammering nails into the loose plank. When he looked up and saw Amelia, he began to roar. "I thought I told you to –" Suddenly, Clodhopper banged his thumb with the hammer! "OW! OW! OW!" he shouted.

Amelia dropped her ball and ran to help the troll. She knelt on the bridge beside him, kissed his thumb better, and bandaged it with her lacy handkerchief.

"Hmmph. Thank you," muttered Clodhopper under his breath. Then he tossed Amelia her ball, which had rolled into the water. "Now, stay away!"

The following day, Amelia and Truffle found themselves by the bridge again. It was a beautiful day and they had decided to have a picnic tea overlooking the beautiful meadow.

Clodhopper was lying on his tummy on the brow of the bridge, fishing in the brook. Truffle barked happily and bounded over to poke his nose in the big bucket that Clodhopper was going to put the fish in.

Suddenly, the bridge gave a creak! With a startled yap, Truffle scampered back on to dry land – but Clodhopper was not quick enough. The wooden bridge snapped in half with a loud CRACK!

Clodhopper found himself dangling from the broken bridge. He could not hold on and he fell – SPLASH – into the water. "Help!" he cried. "I can't swim!"

Quick as a flash, Amelia found a fallen tree branch and held it out to Clodhopper. He grabbed the branch and Amelia pulled him out of the water, on to dry land.

"Why are you so kind to me?" Clodhopper grumbled. "I'm a mean old troll and I'll eat you for my supper!"

Amelia laughed. "I don't think you're mean. A mean troll wouldn't keep such a beautiful meadow."

All that evening, Amelia helped Clodhopper repair the bridge as best they could. In return, he led Amelia and Truffle into the meadow, and let the princess fill her basket to the brim with rosy apples.

Soon, Clodhopper came to look forward to Amelia's visits. Whenever he heard her light footsteps, he would shout, "Who's that trip-trapping over my bridge?"

Then he would jump out to surprise her with a bunch of wild watercress or a pot of honey from the hives. Clodhopper learned how nice it was to share his meadow with friends.

One morning, Amelia arrived at the bridge to see that everything was different.

Clodhopper had taken down all of the signs warning people away. The bridge had been painted a bright apple green, and wild flowers had been tied in bunches to the posts.

In the meadow, the fruit trees were bare, the flowers had all been picked and the beehives were empty of honey.

"Clodhopper has been very busy, hasn't he?" said Amelia with a smile. "But where is he?"

"Clodhopper, are you there?" Amelia called. There was no answer.

As she and Truffle searched along the bank, the little dog spied a tiny path disappearing into the long grass at the water's edge, and scampered off down the track. Amelia ran after him.

Suddenly, Truffle stopped and poked his head into a hole beneath a mound of grassy earth. From inside the mound, Amelia could hear the tinny sound of pots and pans clattering, and a voice shouting, "Put more wood on the stove!"

Amelia peered into the hole.

To her amazement, she saw lots of little trolls, like miniature Clodhoppers in chefs' caps and aprons, running to and fro, stirring pots and lifting lids. Everything smelled delicious.

"What are you cooking?" Amelia asked, surprising the trolls who had not seen her peering in.

One tiny troll spoke up, "Our master has asked us to prepare for a su–" The troll standing beside him gave him a nudge. "A surprise," the first troll said, smiling. "Come to the bridge at sunset and you'll find out what it is!"

That evening, as the golden sun sank low in the sky, Clodhopper led Amelia over the bridge and into the meadow. There, tables were piled high with rosy fruits and honey. "This is your summer ball," said the troll shyly, "the one you thought of when you first saw my meadow."

All of Amelia's friends were there – handsome Prince Fergus, Mr Wolf, Albert the bear and the little woodland creatures, too!

As the trolls played a merry tune on their fiddles, Clodhopper and Amelia danced beneath the cherry trees. Amelia was delighted to have such a kind, new friend.

Magical titles available in this series:

Look out for more enchanting tales to add to your collection!

My *Barbie* Story Library

Barbie Story Library is THE definitive collection of stories about Barbie and her friends. Start your collection NOW and look out for even more titles to follow later!

ISBN: 978 1 4052 3105 3 • RRP: £2.99 ISBN: 978 1 4052 3106 0 • RRP: £2.99 ISBN: 978 1 4052 3107 7 • RRP: £2.99 ISBN: 978 1 4052 3108 4 • RRP: £2.99 ISBN: 978 1 4052 3109 1 • RRP: £2.99

A fantastic offer for Barbie fans!

In every Barbie Story Library book like this one, you will find a special token. Collect 5 tokens and we will send you a brilliant double-sided growing-up chart/poster for your wall!

Simply tape a £1 coin and a 50p coin in the spaces provided and fill out the form overleaf.

STICK £1 COIN HERE

STICK 50p COIN HERE

NOTE: Style of height chart may differ from that shown.

To apply for this great offer, ask an adult to complete the details below and send this whole page with a £1 coin, a 50p coin and 5 tokens, to:
BARBIE OFFERS, PO BOX 715, HORSHAM RH12 5WG

☐ Please send me a Barbie™ growing-up chart/poster. I enclose 5 tokens plus £1.50 (price includes P&P).

Fan's name: .... Date of birth: ....

Address: ....

....

Postcode: ....

Email of parent / guardian: ....

Name of parent / guardian: ....

Signature of parent / guardian: ....

Please allow 28 days for delivery. Offer is only available while stocks last. We reserve the right to change the terms of this offer at any time and we offer a 14 day money back guarantee. This does not affect your statutory rights. Offers apply to UK only.

☐ We may occasionally wish to send you information about other Egmont children's books, including the next titles in the Barbie Story Library series. If you would rather we didn't, please tick this box.

Ref: BRB 001

cut along the dotted line and return this whole page